Charles S. McClenthen

Narrative of the Fall

Winter Campaign

Charles S. McClenthen

Narrative of the Fall
Winter Campaign

ISBN/EAN: 9783337252694

Printed in Europe, USA, Canada, Australia, Japan

Cover: Foto ©Andreas Hilbeck / pixelio.de

More available books at **www.hansebooks.com**

NARRATIVE

OF THE

FALL & WINTER CAMPAIGN,

BY A PRIVATE SOLDIER

OF THE 2ND DIV. 1ST ARMY CORPS,

Containing a Detailed Description of the

"BATTLE OF FREDERICKSBURG,"

At the portion of the line where the 2nd Div. were Engaged.

WITH ACCURATE STATEMENTS

OF THE LOSS IN

KILLED, WOUNDED AND MISSING,

IN EACH REGIMENT.

SYRACUSE:

MASTERS & LEE BOOK AND JOB PRINTERS.

1863.

PREFACE.

The success of "A Sketch of the Campaign from Cedar Mountain to Antietam," has led the writer to a continuation of the narrative in this little work, which he has endeavored to render of more general interest than the other. Information kindly furnished by the Brigade Commanders, has enabled him to give a better and more detailed description of the part sustained by the Division in the battle of Fredericksburg, than he could have done from his own personal observation; and like the Sketch, this Narrative has been submitted to, and received the approval of those best calculated to judge of its truthfulness. With a hope that the fact of its having been written on the march and in camp, subject to frequent interruption and annoyance, may render criticism more charitable, and it may be deemed worthy the same encouragement bestowed upon his former effort, he remains

Your obedient servant,

CHARLES S. McCLENTHEN.
Co. G., 26th Reg't N. Y. V.

NARRATIVE.

During the few weeks of delightful weather which fo
lowed the battle of Antietam, the 2nd, Rickett's Division
of the 1st, Hooker's army corps, lay pleasantly encampe
near the banks of the Potomac, some two miles from Sharp
burg, Maryland, spending the time not occupied in dril
picket, and the other duties of a soldier, in reviewing th
battles and other incidents of the Summer's campaign, di
cussing the merits of President Lincoln's Emancipatio
Proclamation, speculating upon the probable continuanc
of the war, and wondering what was to be done nex
agreeably diversified by baking corn cakes of meal grate
by themselves on old canteens, punctured with the point
a bayonet. In the meantime we had received new clothing
blankets, and other articles necessary to our comfort an
efficiency, and considerable accessions in numbers compo
ed of recruits, convalescents from the Hospitals, and tw
large new Regiments, the 16th Maine and 136th Pa. Th
Division was organized in three Brigades of Infantry, eac
with a Battery of Artillery attached as follows :

The 1st, Duryeas, under command of Col. McCoy of th
107th Pa., composed of the 97th, Col. Wheelock ; 104t
Col. Prey ; and 105, Major Sharpe,—New York Reg
ments ; and the 107th Pa., Lieut. Col. McAllen in cor

mand, to which was attached the Pa. Battery commanded by Capt. Thompson. The 2nd, Tower's Brigade, command-ed by Col. Lyle of the 90th Pa. National Guard; besides which Regiment, under command of Lieut. Col. Leech, there was the 26th, Lieut. Col., now Col. Richardson, and 94th, Col. Root,—New York Regiments; the 88th Pa., Col. McLean, and the then recently added 136th Pa., Col. Bayne, with Hall's excellent 2nd Maine Battery of six Wiard Guns; and the 3rd, Hartsuff's Brigade, commanded by Brig. Gen. Taylor. This Brigade, like the 2nd, had five Regiments, the 11th Pa., Col. Cotter; 12th Mass., Col. Bates; 13th Mass., Col. Leonard; 9th N. Y. M., Col. Stiles, and the 16th Maine. Lieut. Col. Tilden;.. and La-pine's 5th Maine Battery of six brass 12 lb. pieces.

The whole Division, with the exception of some sickness in the 16th Maine which had not yet become acclimated, were in excellent condition, and would hardly have been recognized as the same body of men who reached Hall's Hill, ragged, dirty and dispirited on the night of the 2nd of September previous. It has become almost proverbial among the soldiers that marching orders and bad weather come together, and the occasion of our leaving Sharpsburg proved no exception to the general rule, for on the 26th of Oct., as we were about striking tents, and packing up to march in accordance with orders received, we were visited by a heavy cold rain storm, accompanied by a piercing north-east wind, the first really uncomfortable or disagreea-ble weather we had experienced since the battle of Chan-tilly on the night of the 1st of Sept.

The 1st and 3rd Brigades, as well as the other Divisions belonging to the Corps, marched in this storm, while the

2nd remained on the ground of the old camp until 1 o'clock of the following day, when they took up their line of march through Sharpsburg, back towards South Mountain, near the foot of which we halted for the first night of our march, Oct. 27th. On the morning of the 28th, although the roads were still muddy, the sky was clear and the sun shone out cheerfully as we crossed the mountain at, or near Crampton's Pass, and continued our march through Burkettsville, and turning to the right took the road to Berlin, a little place on the river and rail road, six miles below Harper's Ferry. Just as we were leaving camp at Sharpsburg, an old lady from Pa. came waddling up to us with a large and well stuffed carpet bag in each hand, inquiring for the 6th Pa. Reserves. Upon being told they had marched the day before, and were then probably at Harper's Ferry, which we then supposed our destination, she seemed much disappointed and almost ready to give up. She said she had two sons in the 6th, and had walked all the way from Pa., bringing the two carpet bags filled with cakes, cheese, bologna sausage, onions, &c., which she knew would prove acceptable to them, and now they were gone. She refused all offers from the soldiers to purchase any portion of her load, and upon ascertaining the distance to where we supposed her sons were, concluded to continue her search for them ; so with a soldier on each side of her, who disputed for the privilege of carrying her carpet bags in addition to their already heavy loads, on she trudged with us, affording considerable merriment by the odd manner in which she expressed her strange notions of a soldier's life. Arriving at Sharpsburg, she left us in the hopes of obtaining a ride in some of the wagons or ambulances, enjoining upon us with her last words, if we saw her sons, of whose name or Company we knew nothing, to tell them she was coming. She found her sons I presume, for I saw her a day or two afterwards in Berlin, accompanied by a stalwart Pa. soldier, who I am sure was better pleased with this proof of affectionate solicitude on the part of his mother, than the present she had so kindly brought him.

Upon arriving at Berlin on the evening of the 28th, we found quite an army already encamped there, awaiting their turn to cross the pontoon bridge thrown across the Potomac at that point, and remained until the afternoon of Thursday the 30th. When crossing we marched through Lovettsville three miles from the river, and encamped about the same distance beyond, in the midst of a lovely country a few miles to the eastward of the Blue Ridge, along the side of which we could plainly see our signal stations.

On Friday the 31st, we were inspected and mustered in for pay. Our Brigade, by Col. McLean, of the 88th Pa., who by main strength succeeded in breaking some of our bayonets, which as they are the strongest and best (with the exception of the sabre bayonet) in use in the army, and there was no probability of their being soon replaced, I looked upon as rather mistaken zeal on his part as an inspector. We were also served with three day's rations, and three of us drawing together, received nearly 1 lb. salt pork for the three days, making our allowance less than the 27th part of a lb. to a meal; but as I drew the rations and dislike discussion, I kept all the pork for myself for fear of causing a quarrel in the division. Notwithstanding the liberal allowance made and provided by government for the subsistence of the army, it is an undeniable fact, that the men frequently suffer everything but downright absolute starvation from want of rations. This suffering arises from various causes, the only one of which that could not be easily remedied is the occasional delay in transportation. The others are, the issuing to troops on the march, of rations in larger quantities and for a greater number of days than it is possible for the men to carry in their haversacks, (and which are necessarily left behind them,) for the purpose of lightening the trains and saving the officers of the department the annoyance of more frequent issues; and the frauds and imposition which, although I could not prove, I firmly believe to exist in the Department itself.

Saturday, Nov. 1st. This morning a woman came into camp to complain of some soldiers who had broken into and robbed her house while she was absent for a short time, on the day before. She had two sons in the Union Army, one of whom was then in hospital suffering from wounds received while fighting in defense of our cause, and yet men claiming to be, and wearing the uniform of Union soldiers, were carrying off and destroying the little she had, taking things that were entirely useless to them, merely to gratify their love of plunder and destruction.

I can assert with pride and pleasure, that the vast majority of the army have too much self esteem and conscientiousness to be guilty of such acts; but there is a sufficient number of infamous wretches, who notwithstanding the vigilance of Provost Guards attached to each Division, are constantly committing outrages which detract from the good name of the whole. While in Virginia they always excused themselves by saying the parties plundered are secesh ; but I have seen the same men prying open drawers, destroying valuable papers, breaking mirrors and crockery-ware, stealing childrens' shoes and ladies' bonnets, in the houses of good Union people in Maryland, who were busy with their horses and wagons in bringing our wounded off the battle field ; and who had thrown open their doors, telling the soldiers to help themselves to everything they found to eat or drink. These acts are not committed by the men, who because they swore an occasional oath, made use of ardent spirits, or went fishing on Sunday, were called hard cases at home ; but by men who are totally depraved by nature, and who now, freed from the restraints imposed upon them by society and the laws at home, give full vent to their lawless inclinations and brutal passions. I am sorry to say too, that I have known instances where Company and Regimental officers encouraged pillaging, screening the offender and sharing the plunder. I have spoken of this subject somewhat at length, because in common with all others making any pretentions to decency or respectability, I consider it ruinous to discipline and disgraceful to the service ; and it has nothing whatever to do with the taking of property by the proper departments for government uses, confiscation of property for treason, or any other waste or destruction incidental to the existence of war, and justified by the usages of other civilized nations. I only speak of a system of lawless pillaging in which the sufferers are almost invariably the poor, weak and defenseless, the extent of whose offense against the Government consists in living on the South side of the Potomac, without the means of removing to some more favored locality, while their wealthier neighbors—the instigators and supporters of the rebellion—have vamosed, bag and baggage, leaving nothing but their desolate mansions and broad fields behind them. There are many Quakers in this section of Loudon County, and nearly all the citizens profess to be, and I think really are loyal Union loving citizens. As a proof of this, some two or three Campanies of Volunteers for the Union army have been raised in this vicinity, who are now doing good service as guides, scouts, in the detection of spies and other dangerous persons within our lines, and other duties best performed by those who are acquainted with the roads, inhabitants, &c. The rebels when here last, had taken all the men they found capable of bearing arms, forcing them from their labor in the fields, without giving them time to go to their houses for their clothing.

Between 9 and 10 o'clock in the morning we heard cannonading, said to be in the direction of Union, and marched soon after. Some 4 miles farther on we passed through a little village called Waterford, and continuing our march for a few miles came upon the Leesburgh and Winchester turnpike at Harmony, 26 miles distant from Winchester and 8 or 10 from Leesburgh, when, turning to the right and keeping along the turnpike for about 2 miles, we turned into the fields to the left, and passing what would have made excellect camping grounds, halted at last in as miserable a spot as could have been found within 30 miles of the place, where we remained until Monday, the 3d of November. I had at this time been detailed for duty on the Division Provost Guard, and on Sunday, t' 2d, was placed as safeguard at the house of Mr. Pr of Purcellville, as a little clump of three or four houses on the turnpike was called, and I here learned something of what had occasioned the firing for three or four days previous. It seems Pleasanton's Cavalry with a battery of artillery had been skirmishing with the enemy with variable success for two or three days, until Saturday they had succeeded in driving them from Union, and on through Ashby's Gap where we had heard the last firing. During the fight a shot from our battery had exploded one of the enemy's caissons.

There was at the house three paroled rebel prisoners, two of them having lost a leg each at the last "battle of Bull Run." I held a long conversation with them, and found they were much like our own soldiers, anxious that the war should be ended, and not very particular upon what terms.

During the day Gens. McClellan and Burnside with their respective staffs arrived and took up their quarters at the house where I was for a few hours, when they again mounted and proceeded to the front, Gen. Burnside returning about 10 o'clock at night. The rebels had been fortifying Snickersville a day or two before this, but had now evacuated it, and our forces had taken possession without opposition. While here, I heard a conversation which, as it certainly can do no harm and coincides so exactly with my own opinion, formed without the same opportunities for judging correctly, I gladly repeat. It occurred between the officers of McClellan's and Burnside's staffs, and was introduced by one of them (with the rank of Colonel who formerly held an important position on the staff of Gen. Pope) inquiring of another if he knew when Gen. McDowell's court of inquiry took place. The person addressed replied that he thought it in progress at that time, when the first speaker said he thought it quite probable he would be called as a witness, and continued by saying he thought Gen. McDowell possessed all the requisite qualifications for a commanding General in an eminent degree; that in all the acts for which he had been so widely censured, he had been governed strictly by orders received from the War Department; spoke of his skill and good generalship on the retreat from the Rapidan, and satisfactorily explained many of the charges brought against him by ignorant, prejudiced and irresponsible persons. Among other things, he mentioned McDowell as having always been a warm advocate of doing away with the old established and arbitrary precedence of seniority in rank as necessary for the good of the service, and spoke of the patience and manly forbearance with which he had borne his own supersedure and the repeated attacks made upon him by the Northern press, serving his country through all and in whatever position assigned to him faithfully and to the best of his ability, as an honorable, high-minded man and a true patriot.

On Monday, November 3d, we were again on the move, and leaving the Leesburgh and Winchester pike at Purcellville, turned to the left in a southerly direction towards Fillemont. We had not proceeded far, however, before we turned to the right, taking a road which leads by Sillcotts Springs, crossed the Alexandria and Winchester pike between Snickersville and Fillemont near the latter place, and soon after halted for the night. I here saw some of the strongest Union people I had met with yet, and who were as bitter in their denunciations of the "Southern ragamuffins," as they called them, as ever a Southern family could be of the "Northern mudsills." The man of the family had just returned from Maryland, where he had been since the advance of the Southern army, to escape conscription. They gave me a list of prices of some of the most common and necessary articles, and as they may be of interest I give some of them :

Ordinary sixpenny calico, $1.00 per yard ; women's shoes, $6.00 per pair ; and salt, $11.37 per bushel.

On Tuesday, November 4th, much to the regret of the whole Division, Gen. Ricketts left us. Up to this time he had been constantly with us since the first organization of the Division at Fredericksburg, in the fore part of May previous, under command of Major General Ord. Upon the withdrawal of that officer, while on our laborious and fruitless march to Front Royal, soon after he had assumed command of the Division, the reputation which he had acquired at the first "battle of Bull Run," (where he was wounded and taken prisoner,) his coolness and bravery in battle, kindness and careful solicitude for the welfare of the troops under his command, together with his courteous and gentlemanly demeanor, all combining to gain for him the admiration, respect and confidence of both officers and men. Of the causes for which he left us at this time I am profoundly ignorant, (although I presume it was by his own request,) yet I cannot but deem it a matter of regret that he should separate himself from a Division whose interests and his own seemed so nearly identified, and which still bears his name.

Gen. Ricketts was succeeded in command of the Division by Brigadier General Gibbon, of whom we know but little, although he bears an excellent reputation generally, and is enthusiastically spoken of by his old Brigade in King's Division. Late in the afternoon of Tuesday we marched, passing through Bloomfield, at that time the headquarters of Gen. McClellan, and bivouaced for the night a mile or two beyond.

Wednesday, November 5th, when the Division marched, at the earnest entreaty of a man named Carpenter, near whose house we were encamped, I was left behind as a safeguard until the next Division (Brooks', of Franklin's Corps,) had passed on their road to Upperville. This man had suffered less than most others surrounded by an equal quantity of small stock, still he was loud and bitter in his complaints of the soldiers, and I felt but little sympathy for him when Capt. Whalen, a Division Quartermaster, came and took his two work horses for Government use.

On Thursday, November 6th, I again started on my winding way after the Division, along roads and through lanes, that were so crooked that a person lost all idea of the direction in which we were going, and our notions in regard to the points of the compass became so confused that even the sun itself was looked upon as a doubtful guide, and I was reminded of the story I have heard of the negro steersman of a small coasting vessel, whose master after having pointed out the north star and given him instructions to steer directly for it, went below feeling perfectly secure from mistake or accident. The negro soon after left to himself fell into a deep sleep, during which, the wind veering round, the vessel shifted her course, and he awoke to find himself sailing in exactly the opposite direction from the one pointed out by the captain. He at first looked in vain for the star which was to have been his guide, but discovered it at last directly astern of him, when he called to his master, "Hello, massa, you haf to cum on deck an' show me annudder star, I dun pass dat un long ago." All the roads leading in this direction were filled with troops, trains. &c., Burnside's and Sumner's Corps ahead, and Franklin's almost immediately behind our own, and it was no uncommon thing to find officers and men who had been unable to find their regiments for days.

In my journal of this date I find some remarks in regard to sickness, straggling and demoralization in the new regiments of our Division not very creditable to the solid men of the North, of which they were supposed to be composed; but it was their first long march.; they carried heavier knapsacks and lacked the experience of the older soldiers, and have so nobly acquited themselves on the battle field since then, that I beg their pardon for even this allusion to it. As I pushed forward on my road to Union where I expected to overtake the Division, I overtook on the road a paroled rebel prisoner, whose miserable appearance struck me so forcibly that I cannot pass the incident unnoticed. He was a young man of not more than twenty years of age, and had been taken prisoner and paroled at the hospital in Leesburgh. He was evidently in the last stages of a decline, and although nearly or quite six feet in height would not have weighed more than a healthy child. He still preserved, however, a cheerful hopefulness of spirit which to me was really suprising. He belonged to a North Carolina regiment, and was now following our army in the hopes of finding some opportunity to get through our lines and reach his home near Raleigh to die. as he soon must. Upon my telling him that he would not be allowed to pass our lines except at certain points designated in general orders, he laughed at my simplicity, and said there would soon be a big fight somewhere, when he could manage it easily enough ; and from the fact that Gen. Stuart has since telegraphed to our Quartermaster General from Springfield within nine miles of Alexandria, I have no doubt he did. Upon arriving at what is called Quaker Lane, I found that our Division had gone to the right, and following in the same direction myself, I came upon the Middleburg turnpike at the point where it is crossed by Goose creek, when, after another hour's brisk walking, I saw the Division crossing the Pike but a short distance ahead of me, and was soon again in the ranks with my comrades, having made in two or three hours the whole distance accomplished by the Division since I had been left behind on the day before, although the men had been marched until tired the night before, and started again early that morning. We had now left the Middleburg pike, and were on one to the right, leading to Rectortown on the Manassas Gap railroad, where we had been twice before in the early part of the summer, going to and returning from Front Royal. It had been found expedient on the march to place guards at the houses which we passed and near which we were encamped, as unprotected poultry yards presented inducements to straggling and pillage which hungry soldiers could not well resist, and on this night I was placed at the house of Mrs. Margaret Rector. The Colonel of one of the regiments in Burnside's Corps had stayed at her house on the night previous, and although he had stationed guards about the premises, and some of his men had slept in the stable, some one during the night had stolen his horse, which seemed to please the ladies of the house very much, who supposed he had been mistaken for their own. I here had an opportunity of conversing with a lady, the daughter of Mrs. Rector, and aunt to Gen. Rust (formerly in command of Fort Pillow) and Capt. Rector, (killed at the last Bull Run,) both of the Confederate army. She was remarkably well posted in most of the incidents of the war, and perfectly familiar with all the specious arguments used by the secesh in justification of their rebellion, which she put forward with great adroitness; but she confidently asserted, and I have no doubt really believed, that the whole force of the rebels in Maryland at the time of the battles of South Mountain and Antietam, did not exceed thirty thousand, which I mention as a specimen of the egregious falsehoods circulated by the rebels to give hope and encouragement to their friends and supporters. She said the rebel and union soldiers were just alike—they all robbed her whenever they had the opportunity ; yet she was very kind to our men, giving them bread, milk, potatoes, &c., cheerfully, and laughed heartily at some who had engaged her in conversation in front of the house, while others were stealing her chickens in the rear, before we arrived.

Friday, November 7th. Up to this time we had been blessed with as delightful campaigning weather as ever gladdened the heart of a soldier, but now the scenes were suddenly shifted, and instead of the clear, bracing weather which had rendered our march so pleasant so far, we were treated to a severe snow storm as an inkling of what we might expect during the coming winter. We marched all day in the storm, passing through the little village of Salem, and thirteen miles farther, the larger and prettier one of Warrenton, for the third time, and encamped not far from our old camping grounds at that place. At Salem, I sought shelter from the storm for a short time in a little church that stood by the roadside, and was somewhat amused by writing done on the walls by the soldiers of both armies. Some of it was in the form of question and answer, like the following: " Who run the Yankees out of Salem?" Ans. " The Texas boys." Under which, evidently of a later date, was, " Who give the Texas boys h—ll at South Mountain?" Ans. " Hatch's Brigade," &c., &c. Over the pulpit was a charcoal sketch of Jeff. Davis, hung by the neck, which, from the names inscribed near it, I supposed to have been executed by some of Blenker's Germans ; and on the road between here and Warrenton we passed the house formerly occupied by Mr. Frank Smith, where, in the spring, Robert E. Scott, Esq., an eminent lawyer of Warrenton, and a staunch Union man, had been killed in an attempt to arrest two s ragglers or deserters from the same Division, (Blenker's.) Warrenton, notwithstanding the gloominess of the weather, seemed to wear equally as lively an air as upon our two other visits to it during the summer. The streets were filled with officers and men, among whom might be seen many invalided rebel soldiers; and the surgeons left in charge of them.

Our advance into this portion of Va., at this time seemed to have taken them by surprise, most of them having supposed the Union army would go into winter quarters along the line of the Potomac, while their's would occupy nearly the same position as the winter before. On the afternoon of Saturday, the 8th Nov., Hartsuff's, or rather Taylor's Brigade, marched for Rappahanock Station, on the Orange & Alexandria Rail Road, from which our cavalry and a Battery of artillery had driven the enemy on Friday night, taking a few prisoners, and with a few judiciously distributed shells, forcing those encamped on the other side to skedaddle in the most approved style, leaving their tents, camp equipage, &c., behind them. These remained standing where they were for several days, the enemy making some slight demonstration as if to retake them ; but a wholesome dread of our artillery prevented their doing this, and at last Col. Colter of the 11th Pa., in pity for the annoyance they must feel in seeing their property still there without daring to approach it, went over with his Regiment and brought their traps to our side of the river.

On the march and while at this place, I saw many men that had been wounded, but were now convalescent, paroled prisoners and others on their way to rejoin their Reg. iments, some singly, others in squads, and quite a body of them brought up the rear under an escort or guard of cavalry, and were turned over to the Provost Marshals, to be sent to their respective Regiments. A large proportion of this number doubtless were worthless skulkers and stragglers, who fully deserved the treatment they had received ; but among them were men whom I knew to be faithful, zealous soldiers, whose statements were entitled to the fullest credence, and for the sake of these and such as these I devote space to a brief account of the convalescent camp misery, at Alexandria, as received from them, in the hope that it may meet the eye of those in whose power it is to prevent a continuance of the abuses mentioned. Wounded in battle they had been sent to hospital, and from thence, when sufficiently recovered, to the convalescent camp to await an opportunity of rejoining their Regiments. Here it seems those newly arrived are formed in line daily, and their own statements taken as to their ability to do duty, the honest, faithful man in his anxiety to return to his Regiment, perhaps professing to be better than he really is, is immediately sent to the camp of stragglers, deserters, and other bad characters, to await the departure of a squad to that portion of the army to which he belongs. Here the quarters are represented as miserable and filthy in the extreme, and he is sent daily to work under a strong guard like a convicted criminal, remaining in some instances in this situation for weeks, when he is again sent under guard to join his Regiment, exasperated and demoralized by the treatment he has received. On the other hand the habitual shirk pretends to some ailment, and remains with good food and quarters, under the treatment of the Surgeons. In the case of those who rejoined us at Warrenton, they had been sent from Alexandria to Harper's Ferry, and started from there, with only one day's rations, to follow and over-take their Regiments in the front, which they did after a march of over sixty miles, making twenty-two miles without rations on the last day, some of them unable to keep up, having been brutally maltreated by the guard of cavalry which accompanied them. I myself saw a General of the Union Army borrow a waggoner's whip, and apply it to the back of one of them who, goaded to desperation, and whose physical debility was sufficiently proven by his appearance ,had made him, what was construed as an insolent reply, with as little mercy as would have been bestowed upon a baulky mule.

I here also give a brief, but authentic history of the "Virginia Black Horse Cavalry" (of which so much has been said and written, with so little truth), obtained from citizens of Warrenton, whose acquaintance I had formed years ago, while temporarily a resident of the place. It was first organized in this (Fauquier) County some years ago as a Volunteer Cavalry Company, and was composed mostly of the gentry of the county, candidates for admission being elected by ballot, and exercised no small influence upon the local elections and other matters of public interest throughout the county. During the excitement caused by John Brown's raid at Harper's Ferry in 1859, it received a new impetus and some accessions in numbers, but has never numbered more than from 130 to 150 members. It was commanded at the commencement of the war by Capt. John Scott, who upon leaving it to take command of a troop of partizan cavalry, was succeeded by W. H. Payne, of Warrenton, who has since been promoted to Major of some other organization, and whom I saw in Warrenton last summer wounded and a paroled prisoner. The troop is now commanded by Capt. Charles Randolph ; and if we except the first battle of "Bull Run," where they are said to have charged upon some of our troops when they were in full retreat after the rout became general, have not been in any engagement during the war, and have lost but two men killed (Gordon and Tyler), who were shot through mistake 'by the pickets of a South Carolina Regiment. They have been doing duty most of the time as body guard to Gen. Ewell or some other, their horses are not, and never have been generally, black, and they are simply a very good body of gentlemanly "feather-bed soldiers;" an excellent illustration of the "great cry and little wool" stories so common at the present time.

On Sunday, the 9th November, salutes were fired, and the troops turned out for review, upon the occasion of McClellan taking his farewell and Burnside assuming command of the army. At this time it was generally supposed by us that Gen. McClellan had been appointed Commander in Chief, and our regret at parting with him in the field, even under these circumstances, was very great; but when it became known that his connection with the army was to cease altogether, the excitement for the time seriously menaced the discipline and morals of the army. Officers threatened resignation, men desertion, and all vented their indignation in curses both loud and deep, upon those whom they thought the cause of or in any way connected with his withdrawal. These feelings soon gave way to the despondency of hopelessness or utter indifference, which in its turn wore off, leaving the officers and men in the performance of their duties with the same cheerfulness, and eating their rations with as good an appetite as if nothing had happened. It is generally the case, that when any great popular favorite is displaced by other means than the popular will, some portion of the regret and dissatisfaction of their friends and admirers finds vent in splenetic denunciation of, and detraction from the merits of their successor; it was not so in this case however, for amid all the regrets consequent upon the removal or withdrawal of McClellan, and the execration of those supposed to have been the cause, there was no objection raised to Gen. Burnside, and there is no doubt but the speedy reconciliation of the army to the loss of the former, was owing to the high estimation placed upon the services, and the perfect confidence then felt in the talent and integrity of the latter.

On Monday, 10th, we again struck tents and marched for Bealltion Station, on the Orange & Alexandria Rail Road, between Warrenton Junction and the Rappahanock. The distance from Warrenton village is but little over nine miles, yet notwithstanding most of the officers and men were familiar with this section of the country, we were marched by a roundabout way at least fifteen miles before reaching the station, which we did at last, tired and out of patience late at night.

I believe there is but little use in my saying anything about the mismanagement, and lack of judgment sometimes displayed by General officers in marching their commands, and the selection of camping grounds for them ; it would do no good, and I am like the man who swore terribly when one or two pumpkins rolled off his load, but when the end board came out, and the whole waggon load went tumbling down the hill together, remained silent ; and when asked why he did not swear then, "Ah," says he, " its no use, I can't do the subject justice."

Upon the march referred to, a little incident occurred, which though slight in itself, served to amuse me, in spite of my ill humor at being marched so far out of our way. It had been found necessary for the prevention of straggling to the front, to send a guard in advance of the Division immediately following the Gen., and upon this occasion I was one of the party detailed for this duty. We had halted for a few moments to rest, the Gen. and staff riding on ahead, when an officer rode up and inquired for Gen. Gibbons, to which one of our number, a new recruit belonging to the 90th Pa., and just from Philadelphia, replied, " Well, I guess he's about three squares ahead."

We remained at Beallton one week, and before marching again there was some changes made in the different Brigades ; the 88th Pa., Col. McLean, leaving us for Taylor's Brigade ; and the 94th N. Y., for Duryeas, of which Col. Root, a young but highly meritorious officer, formerly Lieut. Col. of the 21st N. Y. (Buffalo) Regiment, took command. The 97th N. Y., Col. Wheelock, was also transferred to Taylor's Brigade, while the 16th Maine replaced it in Duryeas' or Root's, and the 12th Mass., a small but excellent Regiment, formerly commanded by Col. Fletcher Webster, was assigned to ours in the place of the two taken, leaving us with four Regiments, while each of the other two have five. Here I was placed on guard at the house of a man who had taken the oath of allegiance, and had Union protection papers which afforded just no protection at all, unless shown at the end of a guard's bayonet, and even then was powerless to protect him from some forms of annoyance. Once while there, a soldier came with a very dull axe, which the old man helped him to grind, turning the stone himself, when to punish him as I suppose, for not having furnished cider, the soldier tried the edge of his axe on one of his finest young apple trees, as he passed it on his way back to camp. At this house I saw a young man who had just returned from Richmond, via. Fredericksburg.

2

He stated there were no troops on the way except in the immediate vicinity of Richmond; and all the citizens in this section seemed much surprised at the reappearance of our army here at this time, believing their own to be still in the valley of Virginia, or somewhere in the rear of us.

We left Beallton on Monday the 17th of November, taking what is called "the old marsh road," towards Fredericksburg; passing through Morrisville and Grove Church we bivouacked for the first night at Deep Run, the line between Fauquier and Stafford Counties, where I saw a man who would prove a great curiosity in any part of the world, but was more especially so in this portion of Virginia, which has always been noted for its fox hunting, horse racing, cock fighting, card playing and whiskey drinking gentry. He was thirty odd years of age, over six feet in height, and declared most positively, in which he was seconded by his wife, that he had never drank a drop of intoxicating liquor, chewed or smoked any tobacco, played or bet upon a game at cards, or indulged in any of the bad practices, not only common, but almost universal in this part of the world. He was passionately fond of hunting and fishing however, had shot an eagle the day before, measuring over eight feet from tip to tip of its wings, and gave me some fresh fish from the Run for my breakfast. He had been drafted under the conscription act, but managed to be absent on one of his hunting excursions when they came for him, and although they had left an order for him to report at Morrisville, he said he had nothing to report and remained at home. In other words "He could'nt see it." He had six hundred acres of good land, a pretty wife, and two healthy good natured children, said he had never done a day's work in his life, and was upon the whole, secesh or union, war or no war, one of the happiest, easiest going fellows I have ever met. I shall not divulge the name of this Virginia non-secesh, as I have some notion of trying to engage him for exhibition when the war is over, and I am afraid he would not escape Barnum as easily as he did the draft.

A thing which struck me forcibly and with surprise was, that in all my conversations with citizens while on the march through Virginia, they invariably spoke of the South Carolina soldiers as the poorest and least to be depended upon of any in the confederate service, and I have heard the same opinion expressed by prisoners of war. The 9th Va. Cavalry was frequently spoken of as an active and efficient cavalry Regiment, but all concurred in the statements already made in regard to the Black Horse Cavalry.

Tuesday 18th, we proceeded on the road to Fredericksburg as far as Hartwood Church, ten miles from Fredericksburg, where we found Burnside's and Sumner's old corps already encamped; and turning to the left took the road towards Stafford Court House, halting for the night seven miles from the Court House, nine from Brooks' Station, and fifteen from Acquia Creek Landing. It rained during the night and next day, and we had not proceeded more than a mile or two on the following morning, before we found the road almost impassable. The soil through this section is a light sandy loom, which, when wet with slight rains makes very good wheeling for light vehicles, but affords no sufficient bottom for the heavy laden supply-trains, ammunition wagons and artillery, which sank almost to their axles in the occasional quicksands along the narrow and crooked road, cut in many places through a dense thicket or undergrowth of young pines. We remained for several hours in a pelting rain, at the bottom of a deep ravine we were obliged to cross, while the pioneers of Doubleday's Division and our own, were trying to make the road up the hill on the other side practicable for the trains, and were forced to leave them behind at last. Ascending the hill and turning to the right, we soon came upon the Pa. Reserves, encamped in a large hollow or basin almost entirely surrounded by hills upon all sides, and went into camp, the wagons not coming up until the next morning. We remained here several days, the first two or three of which it rained almost constantly, pickets were thrown out, and large details were made to work upon the road daily.

Sunday the 24th, we marched to near Brooks' Station on the Rail Road, from Fredericksburg to Acquia Creek, and encamped within half a mile of what had been so pleasant a camp in the Spring.

Upon returning to a place which had been before visited, the mind naturally reverted to the changes that had taken place in the interim, and with us they were many and suggestive. Upon the arrival of our Regiment (the 26th N. Y.) at this place early in the Spring of 1862, after nearly a year spent in drill, working on fortifications, doing picket and garrison duty, we numbered over nine hundred men eager to distinguish ourselves in the field, as we had already done with the pickaxe and spade ; a fact which Forts Ellsworth and Lyon, proud monuments of our energy and zeal as diggers of mud, fully attest. Under command of a Col., whose excellence as a diciplinarian and drill master, together with his fine military bearing, had gained for him our unlimited confidence; assigned to the command of Brigade and Division Generals (Ord and Ricketts) who had already distinguished themselves since the beginning of the war, under these auspices we looked forward to a useful and brilliant campaign, to which those that were spared could point back with pride and pleasure. How have those sanguine expectations been realized? Our Col. has proven himself to be afflicted with a constitutional timidity under fire, that even his pride and ambition for military distinction could not overcome, and which at last forced him to resign under unfavorable circumstances ; and after long, weary marches, upon which we have seen our comrades sicken one by one, and battle fields where they have been killed and wounded by dozens, without eliciting even a passing newspaper remark, we return with less than one-third our original number present for duty ; but moralizing is not my forte, and if I go on in this manner I shall soon be unable to extricate myself.

Soon after our arrival, the trains commenced running from Acquia Creek landing, thus affording us an easy communication with our base of supplies, and the length of time we remained encamped here, during excellent weather for active military operations, led many to suppose we were permanently located here for the winter, and the men commenced building log shanties, digging log cellars, &c., taxing their ingenuity to the utmost, in contriving how they should make themselves comfortable during the severity of the coming winter.

About this time, several officers of one of the Regiments in our Brigade were court marshaled, for having appropriated the private's rations to their own use, which was generally applauded by the men as evidence of the fact, that army regulations applied to officers as well as men, and that we had a General who would enforce them. While at this camp I received six hundred copies of " A Sketch of the Campaign in Virginia and Maryland," the success of which has led me to the publication of this, and I was both surprised and pleased at the avidity with which the soldiers bought and read it. In offering it for sale, I obtained some insight into the character of certain individuals, of which I should otherwise have remained in ignorance. Several of the field officers in the Division had taken quite a number of them, and among others I called upon Col. McLean, of the 88th Pa. He had been absent on sick leave nearly the whole time of which the Sketch treated, leaving the Regiment in command of the Lieut. Col., his brother who was killed at Bull Run, when the command devolved upon Maj. Gial, who was severely wounded at Antietan. The Regiment had lost largely in killed, wounded and from sickness, and had suffered more from want of tents, clothing, blankets, shoes, &c., than any other I had seen in the field ; indeed, I doubt if any Regiment could have been found in the proverbially ragged and shoeless ranks of the rebel army, that would have presented a more destitute appearance than they did for weeks after the battle of Antietam, and until within a few days of our march from Sharpsburg, when the Col. returned.

The Col. was sitting in his tent, when I asked him if I could sell him a sketch of the campaign written by a private soldier ; " No sir ! " said he, " I was all along there, know all about it." He has since ended his military career by resigning before the battle of Fredericksburg. The next was Col. Colter, of the " old eleventh Pa.," an officer who has been present, and distinguished himself upon every occasion where his Regiment has been engaged, remaining on the field in command of his Regiment when wounded in the battle of Fredericksburg ; and whose determined, unflinching bravery on the field, together with his energy and promptness, in seeing that his men are properly provided for, has made him a general favorite with the whole Division. " Yes sir ! " was his ready reply, " buy anything written by a private soldier."

Although the nights were cold, the weather during our stay at Brooks' Station was generally delightful until the 5th December, when we had a cold rain which soon turned to snow, and continued until the ground was covered to the depth of four or five inches, and was followed by several days extremely cold weather, causing me to regret my incredulity as to the length of our stay, which had prevented me from fixing up my tent.

No day is suffered to pass in the army, without the circulation of new and contradictory reports, which are like the wind, no man knowing whence they come ; and at this time they were as plentiful and contradictory as ever—all sorts of stories being told of what other portions of the army were doing, and what was to be done with us. One day the enemy had crossed the Rappahannock, and taken our pickets prisoners in a body ; the next they had evacuated Fredericksburg, and we were immediately to advance by that route to Richmond. Some had heard that we were to be shipped at Acquia Creek to join the army in North Carolina, while others had positive information from authentic sources, that the New York two years Regiments were to be mustered out of the service, and new Regiments fill their places. The old troops paid but little attention to these reports, well knowing from experience, that men in the service can be certain of nothing faster than it actually occurs ; but the new ones were not a little puzzled in trying to believe them all at once. The arrival of the pontoons, however, settled the question, and it became evident that we were to cross the Rappahannock, and give battle to the enemy at or near Fredericksburg ; so on Tuesday, the 9th December, we again packed up and moved in that direction, crossing the Potomac Creek, and halting for the night a short distance beyond.

Wednesday, December 10th. Moved forward on the road to Fredericksburg as far as Gen. Burnside's headquarters, and turning to the left on the road to Belle Plain, went into camp. At night it was reported that we had orders to move, first at 1 and then at 3 o'clock in the morning ; but at 9 or 10 o'clock the pontoons upon which we expected to cross the river were still blocked in the road near our camp by artillery and wagon trains, officers swearing and hallooing at the drivers, drivers kicking and cursing their mules and each other, the mules braying, (or cheering for Siegel, as the boys call it,) making altogether as noisy and discordant an entertainment as ever disturbed the rest of a sleepy soldier. We were awakened on the morning of the 11th by artillery firing in the direction of Fredericksburg ; and as the first faint, gray streaks of the dawn made their appearance in the east, we fell in and took the road towards the river, below the town. Upon arriving at an " old field " just back of the bluffs which overlook the river at this point, we were halted and remained until the next morning. The fire of our artillery, which had commenced before daylight, increasing in rapidity and volume until 9 or 10 o'clock, and was directed upon the town, woods or anything that might afford shelter for the rebel troops within range of our guns on the opposite side of the river, elicited no reply from anything in the shape of artillery; but a small body of sharpshooters in that portion of the town near the river, continued to make their appearance occasionally, firing upon our men engaged in the construction of the pontoon bridges, killing and wounding a number, and seriously retarding the progress of the work, until finding the artillery ineffectual to put a stop to this annoyance, a portion of the 98th New York crossed the river in boats under cover of our batteries, and succeeded in taking the whole number prisoners. With the exception of these men, and two shanghai roosters that were strutting up and down the opposite bank of the river, lustily crowing their defiance of the Yankees, not even the smoke of a single chimney gave evidence that the town was inhabited. How the shanghais, before mentioned, escaped capture with the sharpshooters, I cannot well conjecture, as neither of them showed the white feather. At noon, with the exception of an occasional shot, the firing had entirely ceased, but was renewed afterwards with increased vigor, and kept up until after the capture made by our infantry and the completion of the pontoon bridges. During the day we were also regaled by excellent music, discoursed by the splendid mounted band, attached to Bayard's Cavalry Brigade, which came up after we did, and encamped in the woods

2*

in our rear. The weather was remarkably fine, and, inspirited by the cannonade, suffering neither from want of rations or the fatigue of a long march, the men retired to rest at night in splendid condition, for whatever service might be required of them upon crossing the river next day.

Early on the morning of Friday, December 12th, we fell in and moved to the bank of the river, about a mile and a half below the town, where they had succeeded in completing two pontoon bridges, and were there halted to await the crossing of Smith's (late Franklin's) Sixth Army Corps. Our Division commenced crossing at about 12 M., but when the 3d Brigade (Taylor's) and the 12th Massachusetts, of the 2d, were over we were again halted to allow Bayard's Cavalry Brigade to cross, when the remainder of the Division followed; the 3d Division (Meade's Pennsylvania Reserves) and artillery crossing the lower bridge at the same time. Upon reaching the summit of the bluff on the south side of the river at this point, there extends a gently undulating plain of about a mile and a half in width, through the centre and most elevated portion of which runs the Bowling Green turnpike, in a southeasterly direction, and gradually receding from the river. Along the farthest edge of the plain, and at the foot of a long range of hills, whose wooded slopes afforded a cover for the enemy's infantry, splendid positions for the planting of their batteries, and from which our numbers and position in the plain beneath, were as easily discernable as the moves upon a chess board, runs the railroad to Richmond; the ditches and embankments of which formed the first line of the enemy's works. Their position was well chosen, and a strong one, which, taken together with the fact of their having made no opposition to our crossing after the completion of the bridges, seemed to say, "Thus far shalt thou come, and no farther." There certainly seemed but little prospect of success in an attack, except through great superiority of numbers and the well known excellence of our artillery, which must be attended with heavy loss. After crossing, Bayard's Cavalry Brigade was thrown to the front as skirmishers, to ascertain the exact position of the enemy, and we were marched by a flank in the rear of and to the left of Smith's Corps, which had already formed in line of battle between the Bowling Green road and the river. Each Brigade was massed in column of battalions at intervals of 250 paces ; and we remained for a short time in this position, when the lines of Smith's Corps having been extended on the left, we moved farther down the river to near the large stone residence of Arthur Bernard, halted, and the 2d and 3d Brigades deployed in line of battle, facing eastward and at right angles with the river, the 3d Brigade in front, the 2d (Col. Lyle) in the rear of that, with the 1st Brigade, under command of Col. Root, massed within supporting distance in the rear.

After remaining in this position for some time, we were again moved to the right within 200 yards of the Bowling Green road, and formed an oblique line of battle, with our left thrown forward, and our right resting upon the left of Smith's Corps, the brigades retaining their relative position to each other.

After having taken this position, the 1st and 3d Divisions of our Corps passed in our rear to the left of us and formed lines of battle, the 3d (Gen. Meade) with his right resting upon our left, and the 1st (Gen. Doubleday) on the left of the 3d, with his line extending towards the river, facing eastward.

During the movements I have endeavored to describe, the fog under cover of which we had crossed the river had disappeared, and the rebels had shown themselves cognizant of our presence on their side of the river by a few well-directed shots from one of their batteries, one or two of which seemed to me from where I stood, to fall exactly in the ranks of Doubleday's Division, then to the right of us. They were replied to by our long-range guns on the north bank of the river, and much to my surprise soon ceased firing, a continuation of which must have resulted in considerable loss to some portion of our troops massed upon the plain. About this time I also distinctly saw through the openings in the woods on the hills to the right and in front of us, a body of rebel infantry moving towards their right. While posting pickets in advance there was some little skirmishing, during which some of the 6th Wisconsin, of Doubleday's Division, were killed or wounded; and towards night Gens. Burnside and Franklin, with their respective staffs, passed down to the left, their appearance being greeted by as much enthusiasm as would have been elicited by "little Mac" himself; after which we remained quietly resting on our arms in the position described, during the long cold night which followed, awaking in the morning benumbed and stiff with the cold, to the roar of the artillery as it thundered forth its note of preparation for the hot day's work before us.

On the morning of the 13th, after making coffee and despatching our scanty breakfast, the last one for many a poor fellow, whom the setting sun left stark and cold in death upon that fatal field, we remained as we were until about 9 o'clock, when breaking by the right of companies to the front into column, the 3d and 2d Brigades crossed the Bowling Green road, and advanced into the field beyond and about one-third of the distance from the road to the enemy's first line, when the 3d Brigade, taking advantage of a slight elevation of the ground in front of them, halted and formed an oblique line with their left thrown forward, and the 2d Brigade conforming to their movement, halted about one hundred yards in their rear. The Pennsylvania battery, commanded by Captain Thompson, took up their position upon our right, the Division next us on the left of Smith's corps moving to the rear at about the same time. On our left was the 2d Maine battery; and at the distance of about four hundred yards Meade's Division of Pennsylvania Reserves. In taking this position we were exposed to a heavy fire of shot and shell from the enemy's batteries to the right and in front of us, and were ordered to lie down where we remained for several hours, during which time we suffered considerable loss, that in the 2d Brigade amounting to sixteen killed and wounded. The surface of the earth which in the morning had been frozen hard, was now covered with mud and water several inches in depth, in which the shot and shell which came whizzing, plunging and exploding among us, occasionally killing or wounding some of our number, made it necessary for us to lie close down, rendering our position a peculiarly painful and trying as well as dangerous one.

At a little before one o'clock in the afternoon, the enemy opened fire from two or three batteries they had placed in position on a wooded bluff in front of Meade's Division, and were replied to by the batteries of Meade's, Doubleday's and the 2d Maine (Captain Hall,) of our Division. The firing for a time was terrific; but the enemy having one of their caissons exploded, it was discontinued upon their part, and at about the same time Meade's Division, and the 2d and 3d Brigades of our own, moved almost simultaneously to the front. As we advanced, in addition to the artillery fire to which we were already exposed, we were epened upon by the enemy's infantry from the ditches and embankments of the railroad and the rifle pits in front; but pushing forward to within fifty yards of their first line, Taylor's Brigade halted and commenced firing, as the 2d Brigade, Col. Lyle, moved up, taking position in line with and on the left of them, and also opened fire upon the enemy. During this time the first line of Meade's 3d Division wavered perceptibly, and at last commenced falling back before the scathing fire and overwhelming force of the enemy massed against them, leaving us exposed to an enfilading fire from that direction. We remained thus in the open field, loading and firing, with the terrible and concentrated fire of the enemy's partially concealed infantry and artillery, fast thinning our ranks, until several of the Regiments were entirely destitute of ammunition, orders being sent in the meantime to Col. Root's Brigade, which had hitherto been held as a reserve, to advance to the front and charge the enemy's works with the bayonet. Having unslung knapsacks and fixed bayonets before advancing, they came up in splendid style, the 107th Pennsylvania, Colonel McCoy, 105th New York, Major Sharpe, and the 16th Maine, Lieutenant-Colonel Tilden, in line of battle in front, with the 94th New York, Major Kriss, and 104th New York, Col. Prey, in two parallel lines at intervals of fifteen paces in the rear. Passing over the 26th New York, Major Jennings, and 90th Pennsylvania, Lieutenant-Colonel Leech, who were out of ammunition and had lain down for the purpose, they moved to the front accompanied by the 12th Massachusetts, Colonel Bates, and the 136th Pennsylvania, Colonel Bayne, of the 2d Brigade; but as they first felt the full force of the enemy's fire, their pace slackened, some of the men commenced firing without orders, and it required the combined and most strenuous exertions of the Brigade; Regimental and line officers, assisted by Gen. Taylor of the 3d Brigade, to prevent a halt, which, under the circumstances, must have been attended with the most disastrous results, and continue the advance. Upon regaining the impetus of their advance, and as they neared the railroad, with a shout and a run they cleared the ditches and embankments, waging a hand to hand conflict with the enemy, and penetrated the woods beyond, taking over two hundred prisoners, belonging mostly to North Carolina and Tennessee regiments, of A. P. Hill's Division, among whom was the Lieutenant-Colonel of the 33d North Carolina.

The primary object of the charge at this point was now successfully accomplished, the enemy's first line was broken, their works in our possession, and themselves forced to fall back on their supports, or surrender as prisoners. In effecting this, however, we had suffered serious loss ourselves; as, in their eagerness to engage the enemy, the 94th and 104th New York had broken through the first line, creating considerable confusion, it became necessary to halt and reform before advancing further, if indeed a further advance without supports were practicable.

Colonel Root, leaving his Brigade to be reformed by his Aids and the Regimental officers, now rode to Gen. Gibbon to report progress and receive instructions for his farther guidance. The General congratulated him upon his success so far, and told him to "go on." Certainly, a very concise, definite order, and easily given; but, as the result proved, not so easily complied with. Shortly after this, but not before Colonel Root had again consulted him, Gen. Gibbon was wounded and left the field, the command of the Division now devolving upon Gen. Taylor. The enemy had now rallied, renewing their fire with increased vigor, and notwithstanding the efforts of our batteries by a rapid, constant and well directed fire to prevent it, threatened to outflank that portion of our troops now in the woods, it was found impossible to advance without further reinforcements, and the 26th New York and 90th Pennsylvania, who had retired by command of Colonel Lyle, to a small ravine about one hundred yards to the left and rear, with directions to gather cartridges from the boxes of the dead and wounded, and open fire upon the troops that had followed Meade's Division from the woods, and who were seriously annoying us; now, by order of Gen. Taylor, fixed bayonets and again charged to the front, under a heavy fire from the enemy on the left, and without a round of ammunition in their cartridge boxes. Upon reaching the railroad they were moved by a right flank to where Root's Brigade were still engaged with the enemy, to find them sullenly and reluctantly retiring under a fire that cost many a poor fellow his life who had bravely advanced unharmed, the enemy following no farther than the edge of the woods, but continuing their fire.

We now retired across the Bowling Green road by order of Gen. Taylor. The 94th New York were deployed to the front as skirmishers to hold the field, and details were made from each regiment to go upon the field and collect ammunition from the cartridge boxes of the dead and wounded. About this time Birney's Division arrived upon the field and took up their position near that we had occupied upon first crossing the Bowling Green road in the morning, without the exchange of a shot with the enemy, except by their skirmishers as they were thrown out in advance, relieving ours. Regrets are useless, but I do not believe there was a man in our Division who did not contemplate with painful emotion the result of this day's hard fighting, where we had been eight hours under a heavy and constant fire, and suffered a loss in the infantry brigades of 1,334 officers and men killed, wounded and missing; and what that result might have been had they (Birney's Division) arrived an hour or two sooner, and before we had retired from our dearly bought and bravely won possession of the enemy's first line of works. As we withdrew to the north side of the Bowling Green road, Captain Hall of the 2d Maine Battery, whose loss in men and horses was considerable, was forced to leave one of his pieces on the ground. Upon returning for it with fresh horses, some of them were also killed; but he at last succeeded by the use of prolonged ropes in dragging it off by hand. At dark we received rations and a fresh supply of ammunition, and at about 2 o'clock A. M. on the morning of the 14th, the Division was moved to the left, taking position in the rear of Gen. Doubleday's first Division, where we remained until the army re-crossed the river on the night of Monday, the 15th.

In speaking of the "Battle of Fredericksburg," I have frequently heard the question asked, why the 2d and 3d Brigades were not ordered to charge the enemy's works at the time they first moved forward from the position where they so long remained, lying down under the enemy's artillery fire? But it is extremely doubtful whether a charge at that time would have been attended with the same success as that made by the 1st Brigade, who, notwithstanding the enemy's fire had been materially diminished by that of the 2d and 3d Brigades, were near meeting with a disastrous check. Of the conduct of the officers and men of the 2d Division upon this occasion, it is impossible to speak too highly. There certainly has not been in this, and but seldom occurs in any war, an instance where there is a greater call for cool, determined courage and other soldier-like qualifications; or where that call has been more nobly responded to, and by none more promptly or nobly than the 16th Maine, 1st and 136th Pennsylvania, 2d Brigade, two new regiments, who, in this engagement, were under fire for the first time. By a reference to a table showing the loss in killed, wounded and missing in each regiment, there will be found to exist a great disparity in the proportionate losses of the various regiments; that of the 26th New York, a small regiment, being greater than any other except the 16th Maine, which greatly exceeded it in numbers. I can only account for this by the supposition that the enemy's artillery fire must have been more destructive at some portions of the line than others. Illustrative of this is the **fact that at the time we first crossed the Bowling Green** road in the morning and before we had orders to lie down, one shell exploding in the ranks of the 9th New York Militia, of the 3d Brigade, near the colors, killed and wounded ten or a dozen men at one time. Among the field officers wounded besides Gen. Gibbons, in command of the Division, were Colonel Prey, 104th New York; Major Sharpe, 105th New York, 1st Brigade; Major Jennings, 26th New York, Major Sellers, 90th Pennsylvania, 2d Brigade, and Colonel Colter of the "Old Eleventh Pennsylvania," 3d Brigade, who, with his usual indomitable courage and strength of will, remained on the field in command of his regiment sometime after receiving his wound.

TABLE SHOWING THE LOSS IN KILLED, WOUNDED AND MISSING, OF EACH REGIMENT OF THE SECOND DIVISION, FIRST ARMY CORPS, FREDERICKSBURG, DECEMBER 13TH, 1863.

	KILLED.		WOUNDED.		MISSING.		
	Officers.	Men.	Officers.	Men.	Officers.	Men.	Total.
FIRST BRIGADE.							
16th Maine,..	2	28	8	159	2	32	231
105th N. Y.,.		10	5	157	2	4	178
104th N. Y.,.		·5	8	37		2	52
94th N. Y.,..			4	45		9	58
107th Pa.,...		3	1	46		6	57
Total, ...	2	46	26	114	4	53	575
SECOND BRIGADE.							
12th Mass.,..	1	13	6	80		4	104
26th N. Y.,..	1	28	9	121		11	170
136th Pa.,...	1	10	9	.5		8	110
90th Pa.,....	1	4	2			9	80
Total,.......	4	55	26			32	464

THIRD BRIG

I regret my inability to give an exact statement of the loss in batteries attached to the Division, but it was much larger in proportion than that usually suffered by that branch of the service, owing to their exposed position and the short range from the enemy's batteries. The 2d Maine (Capt. Hall) suffered largely, having one of their caissons exploded, killing a number of men and horses, by a shot from one of the enemy's batteries. Of the nineteen officers present with the 26th New York, besides Major (now Lieutenant Colonel) Jennings, Capts. Shurley, Co. C., Neill, Co. D., Palmer, Co. E., and Lieuts. Jones, Co. A., (also wounded at Bull Run,) Harlow, Co. B., Halsted, Co. C., and Smith, Co. E., were wounded ; Capt. Neill, Co. D., without having received any apparent external injury, being struck totally blind by the concussion of a shell. Adj. William K. Bacon, or " our little Adjutant," as he was familiarly spoken of by the men in reference to his youth and smallness of stature, having recovered from the wound received at Bull Run, and rejoined the regiment while on the march from Sharpsburgh, here received another and fatal wound, and died in the Division Hospital on this side of the river, his early and untimely loss deeply regretted by all who knew him.

On Sunday, the 14th, in company with others, I visited that portion of the field where our Division had fought, to search for the bodies of comrades, some of whom we found and removed to near the river, where we gave them a separate burial, marking their last sad resting place with head-boards obtained from broken cracker boxes, and upon which we inscribed their names, company and regiment, At this time the wounded had been removed to the field hospitals, but most of the dead remained as they had fallen, in almost every imaginable position ; one in particular I passed two or three times without knowing that he was dead, and upon having my attention called to him would hardly believe it until I had asked one of the pickets who was kneeling near him, and in almost exactly the same position. He was kneeling upon his right knee, with his left forearm across his left knee, upon which his head was slightly reclining, and his right hand still grasped his rifle upon the ground, as if just in the act of rising. The bullet that had caused his death had gone entirely through his brain, penetrating his skull in front and coming out at the back of his head. Owing to the near proximity of our pickets to those of the enemy, and the flags of truce almost constantly on the field after the battle, there seemed to be a greater disposition and better opportunities for the soldiers of the belligerent armies fraternizing with each other than ever before ; and notwithstanding occasional skirmishing along the line in which each always accused the other of having fired the first shot, mortifying suggestions of Bull Run from them, and cutting rejoinders of South Mountain and Antietam from our own men, waiting an opportunity to kill each other, and exchanged papers and tobacco for sugar and coffee with great industry, whenever they had an opportunity. This growing intimacy was looked upon with great suspicion by the rebel officers, and with good reason, as it always results, as it did in this instance, in the desertion of more or less of their men, and was at last the subject of very stringent orders from our own commanders, who, I presume, disliked this prospect of having the war settled without farther testing their own skill and good generalship.

I cannot take a final leave of the subject of "the battle of Fredericksburg" without relating a little incident, in the vain hope that my manner of telling it may afford the reader some portion of the amusement its actual occurrence, under my own observation, did me. After the Division had retired to the north side of the Bowling Green road, I saw two stretcher bearers come from the front with a very large, heavy man upon a stretcher, and as they passed near a swampy hollow or ravine, they sat it down and went down into the hollow to get a drink of water. While they were gone, the man upon the stretcher raised himself up, looked around, stood upon his feet, and at last walked off. The surprise of the stretcher bearers at finding him absent when they returned, can better be imagined than described; they looked in every direction, but in vain; their burthen was gone. " What could have become of him ?" said one. " Walked off, I suppose," said the other, " but if I had the big loafer here again " (doubling his fists at the same time) " I'd fix him so he wouldn't git off of another stretcher without help, after our carrying him so far when there want nothing the matter."

There was some artillery firing at intervals during Sunday and Monday, the 14th and 15th, but we suffered no loss, and on the night of Monday, the 15th, we re-crossed the river in the silence and darkness of night, and without annoyance from the enemy, whom I do not believe were aware of our absence until the following morning. No one that was present and witnessed the rapidity, regularity and quietness with which this movement was effected, but must have been forcibly struck with the contrast it bore to the confusion and mismanagement generally attending hurried movements of a large army, even upon occasions where time and good order are equally as valuable and important.

On the morning of the 16th, the whole Division encamped in a large open field to the left of the road running from Fredericksburg to Belle Plain, where upon our first arrival we were visited by some solid shot from one of the enemy's batteries, although the distance from the river must have been at least two miles.

We remained here until Saturday the 20th, when we again marched, and passing White Oak Church, halted near Fletcher's Chapel where, with the exception of some little shifting, and the few days memorable mud campaign, we have remained since. The Brigades are encamped at distances of from half a mile to one mile from each other, within convenient distance of Belle Plain landing, where we obtain our supplies; and with the exception of some difficulty in obtaining wood in the 1st and 3rd Brigades, will, I think, compare favorably as to health, comfort and convenience, with any other portion of the army. The camp of the 2nd Brigade, owing to the careful and judicious selection of Col. Lyle, is certainly in my opinion, the cleanest, healthiest, and most pleasantly located of any in the whole army. Between high wood covered hills, which afford abundant fuel for our fires, and an excellent protection from the bleak chilling winds of winter, winds our little " smoky valley " with a small stream running through its centre, along the banks of which are springs of clear good water almost at our very doors. You need not laugh! I mean doors sure enough, for immediately upon our arrival here, the men were set to work building log shanties, which, with the aid of cracker boxes, and little odd bits of lumber picked up here and there, and in many instances carried miles, and plenty of Virginia mud to fill up the cracks, they have succeeded in rendering tolerably comfortable habitations for the winter. We now resumed our drills and other duties pertaining to a camp in the field, the monotonous routine of which, made familiar to all by the published letters of volunteers, need no mention here.

On the last of December, we were reviewed by Gen. Taylor, and on the 1st of January, Brig. Gen. Robinson assumed command of the Division. We were again reviewed on the 12th of January, and soon after received orders to hold ourselves in readiness, with cooked rations, to march at any time. Details were made to work upon the roads leading towards Falmouth, indicating a move in that direction, with the probable intention of crossing the Rappahannock at some point higher up, and on the 19th, we received orders to march on the 20th ; the old proverb of "marching orders, and bad weather," holding good as usual.

On the morning of the 20th of January, there was neither snow or rain, but gloomy threatening clouds, and a damp, chilly, northeast wind, fully portended the coming storm, as we reluctantly unroofed our comfortable shanties, and made preparations for another march. Between 11 and 12 o'clock we fell in and proceeded as far as "White Oak Church," when we were halted, and orders were read to the different commands, from Gen. Burnside, stating that we were again about to engage the enemy under more favorable circumstances, and when the earnest, active zeal, determined bravery, and patient endurance which were enjoined upon all, were certain to be crowned with brilliant and glorious success. The threatening weather, however, seemed to impress the troops with gloomy forebodings, that even these sanguine orders were powerless to remove, and they were received without any demonstrations of applause or enthusiasm. Neither was there on the other hand, any symptoms of demoralization, there was a willingness and determination to do all that human effort could accomplish to carry out the design of their commander, whatever that design might be, but evidently without any clearly defined hope of success.

And here let me say a few words about the question of demoralization in the army, as I view it from the stand point of a private soldier, after having seen within less than one month of two years service. There has not, is not, nor ever will be any demoralization in the volunteer armies of the United States, in any way calculated to impair its efficiency. The men composing these armies will always have strong preferences for certain Commanders, and their own opinions in regard to the wisdom of the course pursued by the administration in the various campaigns, and other measures for the prosecution of the war ; and they will freely and boldly assert these preferences and opinions, believing that in taking up arms in defense of their country's flag, they are not called upon to resign any of the rights which characterize the American citizen ; but they will at the same time, bravely, patiently, and heroically endure the fatigue and hardship of the march, the tedious monotony of a life in camp, and the appalling dangers of the battle-field, wherever, whenever, and under

3

whatever leaders the properly constituted authorites of their country may deem it wise and expedient to place them.

Upon leaving White Oak Church, we proceeded in a south-westerly direction, sometimes by the road, then across fields, crossing the railroad to Acquia Creek, and on again in the direction of the Rappahannock, at some point above Falmouth. We marched until after dark and halted in an open field, where there was neither wood nor water, just as the threatened storm burst over us. Thick and fast it came, rain, hail, snow and sleet, accompanied by a cold, disagreeable wind, rendering all our efforts to make fires with the little wood we could collect in the dark utterly unavailable. We had neither poles or pins with which to erect our little shelter tents, and were forced to make out the best we could by using our guns, bayonets and rammers instead; but after we did succeed in getting them up after a fashion they were frequently blown down again, and in a short time the whole surface of the field in which were encamped was covered with water, snow and mud, rendering our position the most comfortless I have ever experienced.

I frequently read descriptions of the cries, groans and lamentations of the wounded and dying upon the battle-field, written by persons who were never there; and I passed the night after the "Battle of South Mountain," amid the dead and dying on the most hotly contested portion of the field, but I have never been able to realize the descriptions their imaginations enable them to paint so vividly, as fully as on the night of the 20th of January.

Sick, wounded and dying men have neither strength nor energy to swell their lugubrious chorus of woe to such a pitch as mingled with the howling of the winds, and the merciless pelting of the rain, sleet and snow rose on the midnight air like a chant of despair from the infernal regions. Let no one think I exaggerate in this description; that would be impossible. Danger, disaster, defeat and the fear of instant death could hardly render us more miserable than we were for the time being, through the combination of circumstances described, added to which was the certainty of morning's finding the roads in such a condition as to frustrate the objects of the movement in which we were engaged, and notwithstanding the discomfort and suffering to which we were temporarily subjected. That was the only matter of really serious importance about it, and little incidents were constantly occurring during the night that appealed so strongly to our risibles we " couldn't cry for laughing." Some of the men who had succeeded in getting up their tents immediately upon our first arrival, had spread their oil cloths and blankets and gone to sleep, to be again awakened by the water gradually rising around them, persisted in remaining where they were as long as they could keep their noses out of water, swearing like the gentleman who was refused admission into the ark, there wasn't going to be much of a shower after all. Others whose tents had blown down upon them while they were asleep, had, upon awaking confused and bewildered, become inextricably entangled in them, and now crawling, tumbling and rolling about, enveloped in their thoroughly saturated tents, reminded one in the darkness of the frolicsome gambols of a young hippopotamus. Another who, with misplaced confidence in his own security, had partially undressed himself before lying down, might now be seen shoeless, coatless and hatless in the storm, holding up his tent and hurrying his comrade, who is on his hands and knees in the mud, trying to re-fasten the pins, like the fellow who held the bear while his friend went home for an axe with which to kill him.

Morning came at last, but with it no abatement of the storm; and, although after wringing and folding our blankets and tents, we still continued our march in the direction of the day before, it soon became apparent that all efforts to move artillery or the supply and ammunition trains in the then existing state of the roads would be utterly futile; and after crossing the road running from Falmouth to Catlett's Station, we were halted in the woods beyond, where we remained encamped until we received orders to return to our old camps, at which we arrived on the night on the 23d. Any attempt at description on my part would fail to convey any adequate idea of the state of the roads at this time. I have seen twenty horses hitched to one piece of artillery, where it had sank in the mud until the axles and even the piece itself rested upon the surface. Our own trains never came up with us during the four days, and although they had not proceeded as far as ourselves, did not succeed in returning to camp for two days afterward.

Shortly after our return to camp, where we soon re-fitted our shanties, the 90th Pennsylvania and 210 men of the 136th Pennsylvania, 2d Brigade, were detailed for duty at the Landings, leaving the 26th New York, 12th Massachusetts and remainder of the 136th Pennsylvania, to furnish the same detail for picket in their turn, as the other two brigades of the Division, with five regiments in each, and in some instances it has taken every available man in the 26th New York, including pioneers, officers, waiters, &c., to fill this detail, the frequent recurrence of which during the severe winter weather has been the greatest foe to our comfort. The 90th and the detail from the 136th have now been recalled, and five companies of the 26th New York are now doing fatigue duty at what is called the "New Landing," where, as I am one of the number, I hope they may remain until their term of service expires, on the 2d of May, to which period we are looking forward, with the eager anticipation of being then able, for a time at least, to re-visit our friends and homes.

Entered according to Act of Congress, in the year 1863 by

CHARLES S. McCLENTHEN,

In the Clerk's Office of the District Court, for the Northern District of New York.